Hocus Focus Hullabaloo

Strange and Fantastical Myths and Tales

Chris Firth

This edition published by Electraglade Press – 2014
electraglade@aol.com

First published version by Solomon Press as 'Hocus Pocus Hullabaloo'.

This edition with additional stories is published as 'Hocus Focus Hullabaloo' with the cooperation and support of First Class Learning Ltd, UK, who have rights to use the material as part of educational resources packages.
www.firstclasslearning.co.uk

All rights reserved.
No part of this publication may be reproduced, copied, stored in a retrieval system, transmitted or performed in any form without the prior written permission of the author and Electraglade Press.

Cover and interior design - Electraglade
Cover image - 'The Reptile' - Electraglade
Interior images courtesy of The Pepin Press/Agile Rabbit Editions –
'5000 Animals'

The author would like to thank *The Fortean Times Magazine* for many years of awe, wonder, smiles and inspiration.

Hocus Focus Hullabaloo
ISBN 9781500128494

Hocus Focus Hullabaloo

Strange and Fantastical Myths and Tales
Contents:

Modern Myths
Red Toad
Hat Box
Dominic and Juliet
The Dress

Real Weird
Bad Hair Days
London Underground
Sleepers
Toxic Sludge Mutants

World Wide Myths
The Swan Children of Lir (Ireland)
The Birth of Garuda (Hindu)
King Perun the Tongueless (Eastern Europe)
WWF Minotaur   (Ancient Greek)

Weird Tales
Wondermites
Mal-Beast – The York Golem
Pad-Pad
The Incredible Expanding Reptile
Cracks

MODERN MYTHS

RED TOAD

This uncle of mine, Uncle Jim, just came back from Ethiopia, and he's been a bit sick. He's an engineer, and was working on a project over there, helping to build a dam up in the mountains. He's worked with charities like OXFAM for years, so he's been all over the world with them, but he'd never been to Ethiopia before. He was there right through the rainy season, so there was a lot of water about, along with all sorts of frogs and poisonous reptiles.

I don't know if you've been over there yourself, but if you have you'll know all about the red toads. Those tiny, crumpled warty things that have razor sharp teeth and a nasty little bite. They're only about as big as the end of your thumb, but they're carnivorous and they eat anything that moves. In swarms, they've even been known to attack farm animals and even humans, slithering all over them, eating them alive.

Well my Uncle Jim wasn't that unlucky - he just got a bite on the leg. While he was out working a red toad got down his boot and had a go at his calf. He didn't even realise that it was a bite. He just thought that he'd got a blister or something, but when he got back to his tent that night he took off his boot and out dropped the toad. There was blood all over the back of his leg, a big hole chewed out.

He didn't bother having the wound treated there though; he was due back here the next week so thought he'd wait and see how it went. He just slapped a bandage on, got on with his work, and thought nothing more about it. The bite scabbed over nicely and seemed to be healing fine.

Once he got back here though his calf became swollen and painful. This horrible pus - sticky stuff that looked like pink jelly - started to seep out through the scab. A few weeks later and his leg right up to the knee joint had bloated up like a balloon. He'd been to the doctor's a couple of times but she'd just prescribed antibiotics, which weren't working. Worried that he had caught leprosy, or gangrene, Jim arranged an appointment with a tropical disease specialist.

When he got down to the hospital the specialist felt and prodded the red, swollen leg, humming and muttering, shaking his head. He said that he needed to extract a tissue sample from inside the leg, then gave Jim a local anaesthetic. When the leg was nice and numb, the specialist got to work with his scalpel. He had just sliced in, a tiny little nick, when Jim screamed in agony. From ankle to knee, like a pair of old trousers ripping along the seam, his leg just burst open and thousands of minute baby toads came spilling out over the hospital floor, thousands of them, all red and squirming, trying to hop away from the brightness of the hospital lights. That red toad had laid its spawn in there, you see. The thing had been down Jim's boot all day, filling his leg up with microscopic toad spawn, and in time the spawn had incubated then hatched inside his leg.

Well, that experience was bad enough, and even though Jim's leg healed up nicely, he's still not right. He's turned really weird. He's started slouching about with his legs bent at the knees, his feet pointing outwards. Even his skin's changed too - gone all rough and scaly, with little red warts crowding over his hands and arms. Between his fingers there's skin growing and I swear, when he spreads his fingers now it looks as though he's got webbed hands. Even the local kids have noticed the change in him, and it's embarrassing to walk down the street with him these days. He sort of hops along beside you, like a human toad, with all these kids following and shouting out: 'Red toad! Red toad!'

It's sad, I know, but Jim's so bad these days that even though we love him, warts and all, none of the family will be seen in the street with him anymore. To be honest, we can't wait until he gets off abroad again. The way he's been treated just makes me hopping mad.

HAT BOX

My Auntie Sarah never drives anymore. Not since the incident with the nun and the hat box. She will not even get into a car and starts shaking just at the thought of driving. She used to drive everywhere in a big Rover, a beautiful car that was her pride and joy. Every week day she drove to work and back, a journey of about forty minutes over the moor road between Ilkley and Leeds.

Sarah had made a rule never to pick up hitch-hikers or people trying to thumb a lift, basically because there are so many lunatics about. You don't get many hitch-hikers between Leeds and Ilkley or anywhere these days, but one wet and windy day as she set home from Leeds, Sarah saw a hunched nun trying to thumb a lift on the by-pass. Feeling sorry for the old dear, who was being buffeted by the howling wind and soaked with rain, Sarah broke her rule and pulled up beside the nun. She wound down the passenger window and shouted, 'Where are you heading, Sister?'

'Ilkley, my dear,' croaked the nun, in a voice that already sounded hoarse.

'So am I. Hop in. I'll give you a lift.'

It was all done in a few seconds. The nun was in the car. The doors were closed. They were pulling away into the traffic. The nun, who seemed huge now that she was in the passenger seat, had no luggage apart from a red velvet hat box. This she set at her feet, then hunched away toward the window, face angled away from Sarah. The nun stared out into the gloomy darkness and remained silent.

'Bad night for travelling, isn't it?' said Sarah. She was trying to make conversation, thinking that surely a nun would have something interesting to say.
'Hmm,' grunted the nun.
'Been trying to get a lift there for long?' tried Sarah.
'Hmm,' grunted the nun.
'Oh well, we'll soon be there. And at least the car's warm.'
'Hmm,' grunted the nun, then shuffled in her seat, angling her face even further away toward the window, obviously not interested in making small-talk or having a conversation.

There was an awkward silence in the car. They were out of Leeds and on the moor road when the nun coughed. It was a strange, grating cough. *A smoker's cough?* thought Sarah. And Sarah was sure that she could smell stale beer and tobacco. She thought it odd that an old nun should be a smoker and drinking alcohol. She glanced at the nun's hands which were clasped on her lap, trying to see if the fingers were nicotine stained. They were gnarled, big knuckled, hairy hands. The nun's feet were now resting on the hat box. Instead of the dainty little flat-soled black nun-shoes that Sarah had been expecting there were two huge, muddy brown boots. Sarah was almost in a panic, but she kept her cool and drove on. She sneaked a glance at the nun's reflection in the car windscreen. The nun's eyes were blazing with madness, and there was a strange smile curled on her face - a face that definitely had a touch of blue stubble. There was no doubt about it - the nun was a man. A mad man!

Sarah tried to remain calm, though her stomach was churning in a panic. She said nothing. Now and again as she drove on she lifted her foot from the gas-pedal so that the car sounded as though it was losing power.

'Damn - the electrics,' she cursed. 'Power keeps fading. I've just had it fixed as well. That garage is useless.'

She slowed at the side of the road then stopped.

'Oh hell! Do me a quick favour, Sister. Just nip out and check my back lights, would you? Just tell me if they dim when I rev the engine - I don't want anything running into the back of me.'

The nun grunted something in a muffled voice, but did open the door. She stepped out of the car and walked to the rear of the vehicle. Sarah slammed her foot down and screeched away, leaving the nun standing there in the wind and the rain on the middle of the wild moors. She stopped for a few seconds to close the passenger door, her heart thumping, knowing that she was lucky to escape with her life. She noticed that the mysterious hat box was still in the car, but that was no problem - she would leave it at the police station when she went to report the incident.

Safe in Ilkley, Sarah drove straight to the police station. She was shaking with shock as she climbed out of her car with the hat box. The box was quite heavy, so she rested it on the car bonnet while she made sure her doors were locked. Despite being a bit muddy from the nun's boots, the box looked lovely with its little silver clasp. It was obviously expensive, and Sarah couldn't resist having just a little peek. She undid the clasp and lifted the box lid. Screams of horror shrilled out into the night. When the police rushed out of the station they found Sarah slumped on the pavement where she had fainted. The box was on the car bonnet, the lid still open. Inside the box... the staring, severed head of the nun's last victim.

DOMINIC AND JULIET

Dominic and Juliet met at the dentists. They were both there to have teeth-braces fitted. Recognising each other from school, they smiled nervously across the crowded waiting room. Both winced at the whine of the drill and the screaming from behind the surgery door. Dominic's dad was frowning angrily, and Juliet's mum was scowling.

'If I'd known that old battleaxe was going to be here I'd have arranged another day,' Dominic's dad muttered, meaning Juliet's mum.

'Look at the silly fool, sitting there as though he owns the place," hissed Juliet's mum, meaning Dominic's dad. 'I can't stand that family. They think they own the town.'

It seemed that their parents had met before, and didn't like each other one little bit. But Dominic and Juliet were not really listening. They were shyly gazing into each other's eyes, both smiling sweetly like two star-crossed lovers. Juliet thought that Dominic looked so cute out of his school uniform, like a lovely teddy-bear with his big sticky-out ears. Dominic knew that Juliet lived on the estate somewhere near his own street, and every time he'd ever seen her he'd thought she looked gorgeous. To him, even her spots and blackheads seemed beautiful. Right there, in the grim dentist's waiting room, they fell madly in love.

A week later they met again, this time in the school dinner queue. They smiled helplessly at each other, both mouths glittering with the wire and metal of their newly fitted braces.

'How's your brace?' Juliet asked, keen to break the ice.

'It's fine,' Dominic said, sucking on his brace that filled with spittle in the gaps whenever he spoke. 'Food gets a bit stuck in it, especially chips. They get squashed right into all the corners. It's comfortable though. How about yours?'

'Oh, mine's great. I even sleep in it - it's fixed in. Look, I've got these special screws....'

There in the queue they gazed into each others mouths, comparing brace experiences. They sat and ate lunch together, testing each other's food to see what got stuck in their braces the easiest. By the bell to end lunchtime they were going out, and had arranged to walk home together.

On the way home Dominic told Juliet what his dad had said about her mum in the dentists. She told him what her mum had said about his dad.

'Seems like they don't get on,' Juliet sighed.

'Great. Feuding folks! I'd walk you to your door but...'

'Yeah, maybe another time. We'll have to work on them.'

They parted on the corner with a quick lip-peck of a kiss, both worried that their parents might spot them together. They went their ways, homeward, hearts singing with their new found love.

They went out in secret for weeks. Every night they walked home hand in hand, parting at the corner with a sloppy lip-peck. Both tried to sound their parents out about their hatred for the other family, but neither could get to the bottom of it. It seemed that their grudge went way back to when they were at school together, and Juliet suspected that her dad had at some point gone out with Dominic's mum, but neither could get the whole story. So they sneaked about, meeting here and there in secret, but were never able to really spend much time together.

That term there was a 'Valentine's Day' school disco, and it was the first time that Dominic and Juliet had managed to be together for longer than their short walk home. Juliet's parents had arranged to meet her outside the front of the school when the disco finished at 9pm, as had Dominic's. It seemed that their paths were about to cross once more. The lovers had two whole hours together. They chatted. They cuddled. They lip-pecked. She stroked his ears. He thought how beautiful she looked with the make-up layered over her spots. They even had a dance to the slower music, a smooch, waltzing around like two old age pensioners, clutching and clinging together. Everybody was sniggering at them, but they were so much in love; they just didn't care what anyone thought.

'We'll have to tell our parents - I can't stand all this being apart,' Dominic moaned.

'Soon,' Juliet replied. 'Not tonight though. I couldn't stand a row with the oldies after such a lovely night. Now shut up and snog me.'

'Snog?!'

'Yes. I'm fed up with lip-pecks. Tonight's the night. I want a real kiss.'

Dominic was in a bit of a panic. Like most boys of his age he'd never had a full snog before. He tried to remember all the girls' pop magazine 'problems pages' that he'd sneaked looks at in the newsagents, and all the internet information about how to kiss properly he'd surfed. How would he breath? What would he do with his tongue?

'You want me to snog you here? In front of everyone?'

'Yes, Dominic. I want the whole wide world to know of our love!'

There on the dance floor, with the lights and soft

music, they embraced even tighter. Their lips met; mouths opened; wire braces brushed. They kissed passionately. They snogged most ferociously. They snogged and they snogged. And they snogged. It seemed as though they would never stop snogging. Even when the lights went on and one of the teachers tapped them on the shoulders they went on snogging.

Juliet's dad parked out front of the school at one minute to nine.
    'Must have been a fight or something,' he said, nodding to the ambulance which was outside the school's main entrance. His wife clucked and tutted.

Dominic's mum pulled up outside the front of the school as the clock struck nine.
    'Oh, I hope there hasn't been a fire,' she said, nodding to the fire engine that was parked in front of the ambulance.

Both sets of parents found themselves next to each other in the small crowd that had gathered at the back of the ambulance.
    'It's them!' Dominic's dad hissed to his wife, looking away.
    'It's her!' Juliet's mum snarled. 'Don't dare look at her, you!'

Just then a loud cheer went up from the group of kids around the school entrance.

'Make way... make way...' boomed a tall fireman, cutting-gear and saws in his hands. With one of the ambulance crew he was carefully leading someone through the crowd. The crowd parted. Two sets of parents moaned in horror.

'We'll need their parents to come in the ambulance with us,' a medic shouted. 'These two need a surgical separation, and both sets of parents will have to sign the authorisation.'

There, for all the world to see, face to face, lips still touching, came Dominic and Juliet. They were shuffling along sideways like a huge, weird crab, their gaping mouths locked, tangled together by the wire of their braces. Although they were obviously in some pain, it looked as though they were smiling as they clambered into the ambulance with both sets of parents trailing awkwardly behind them.

THE DRESS

Poor Sylvia, she was beautiful with big green eyes and a perfect mouth, but she never seemed to look right. Although tall and slim, her trainers were Nicks, not Nike. She didn't have a Kappa T-shirt, or her belly-button pierced. When the other girls had their hair cropped modern-short and spiky, she kept hers shapeless and long. Although teased by her mates for being 'sad' and a 'scruff', she just didn't care. She was happy with herself and the way she looked.

Sylvia lived with her mum, who worked hard to keep the two of them going. Dad had left them years ago. There was never much money to spare. The last thing she wanted was to worry her mum with name tags on stupid clothes. But when Lord Rangecroft-Junior pulled up at the school bus stop in his Porsche and handed out invitations for his annual summer ball, held at the hilltop manor house, Sylvia was thrown into a real dilemma. Rangecroft-Junior was the town's heart-throb. He was only eighteen, painfully good-looking, and the heir to millions as well as a title. He was thought to be a better catch than Prince Harry by the rich girls. Not only wealthy, intelligent and handsome, he was a kind person too. He made a special point of presenting an invitation to Sylvia, complimenting her on her beautiful hair and individual looks as he did so.

'Promise me you'll come and have at least one waltz with me,' he pleaded. She smiled shyly and took the invitation. *Formal Attire*, it said. At the manor house that meant a ball-gown.

'I'll try and come,' she lied, knowing that no way on earth could her mum afford a ball-gown. After Rangecroft-Junior had driven away, the other girls teased Sylvia about his attentions to her, but only because they were jealous - even they could see that he fancied her.

'But what will she wear? Jeans and a scruffy T-shirt?' one of them shrilled. The others tittered, glad that somebody had got a dig in. 'Yeah – and she'll be turning up in a pumpkin with those Nick trainers on,' someone else jeered. Sylvia rolled her big green eyes and slipped the invitation into her school bag.

That evening, as Sylvia took out her homework, the invitation slipped from her bag onto the table.

'Hello. What's this, pet?' her mum said, picking up the posh-looking invite. Sylvia sighed and explained about the ball, and Lord Rangecroft-Junior's invitation

'I don't want to go though,' she said. 'It'll be dead boring, and I don't have a dress. I'll just stay home and read my book.'

Her Mum stared down at the card, admiring the gilt border and the fancy, swirling font.

'Don't you worry, pet,' she crooned. 'You'll be going to that ball. By hook or by crook, I'll get you a dress to die for.'

The next day, Sylvia's mum took some of the money she had managed to save out of the bank and went into town. She returned home that teatime with a brown paper parcel, which she dropped onto the kitchen table where Sylvia was doing her homework.

'There you go, pet,' she said. 'One ball-gown. I admit, it's not brand new. It's from Sammy's Seconds. But he swears on his mother's grave it's only been worn once, and it's ever so lovely. You shall go to the ball.'

Sylvia gasped when she held the dress against her body. It was absolutely beautiful – pale blue silk, full length with a fitted waist and pearl buttons. When she tried it on the dress looked perfect, as though it had been made for her. The only problem with it was that it had a strange chemical smell, as though it had been stored for a long time in moth balls. A splash of perfume would take care of that though.

'Mam, this is just so lovely,' she said. 'I feel just like Cinderella!'

'Well, as long as you're home from the ball by midnight,' chuckled her mum, eyes twinkling, happy that her daughter looked so drop-dead gorgeous. Together they did her hair and her make-up, sprayed on perfume to cover up the smell of the dress, then phoned Mickey's Cabs to order a taxi. Off she went, with a last wave and beaming smile from her happy mum.

Heads turned when Sylvia stepped shyly into the ballroom at the Rangecroft manor house. With her hair piled in ringlets, her face shining, and that beautiful blue dress, she looked stunning. Every young man in the place, and especially Rangecroft-Junior, wanted a dance with her. Dancing and chatting, sipping on drinks, time passed in a happy blur. She was having the time of her life, although the continuous dancing made her perspire a little bit. After a while, she even began to feel slightly ill and thought that it might have been because of all the dancing, or the sweet snacks and creamy vol au vents. Rangecroft-Junior, noticing that the girl of his dreams looked slightly pale, led her to the seats which were arranged around the polished dance floor. Sylvia leant toward him and whispered that she felt faint, that she needed air. As he escorted her toward the veranda to get some fresh air, she collapsed into his powerful arms. She had fainted. Rangecroft-Junior and his servants tried to revive

Sylvia but her pulse was very faint, her breathing erratic. People began to panic. Poor Sylvia, there was no reviving her. She was rushed into hospital but never recovered from her fainting fit. Dressed in silk, her hair in ringlets, she died that evening, just a minute before midnight.

Although foul play was not suspected, a few days later the local police called round to see Sylvia's distraught mother. They were kind with her, and gentle, but kept asking her questions about the dress. Where had she got it from? How had Sylvia come to be wearing it? Did it come with any jewellery? It was vital that she told them all about the dress.

Between sobs, Sylvia's mother told them where she had bought it - 'Sammy's Seconds', the shop on the High Street. The shop that sold only guaranteed high quality second hand goods and specialised in original fakes.

Second Hand Sam was interviewed, and on the strength of his statement was arrested - although not for murder. Grave robbery was the crime that he was charged with. Sylvia's post-mortem showed that she had died from poisoning. Her blood had been poisoned by a peculiar fluid that was usually used for the embalming and preserving of human corpses. The dress that she had been wearing had originally been the funeral dress of a wealthy woman from a nearby town. After the woman's funeral, Sammy, or one of his many assistants, had removed the dead woman's dress, along with her jewellery, then sold the haul on through his shop. Apparently they did this sort of thing all the time and had made a fortune out of grave robbery. But this fatal silk dress had been soaked in the toxic embalming fluid before being put on the woman's body. Nobody had thought to wash it out. As the evening of dancing had progressed at the ball, Sylvia's perspiration had caused the fluid to soak from the dress onto her skin, and so through into her bloodstream. Slowly but surely, she had been poisoned through the happiest hours of her life.

Poor Sylvia, she was so beautiful. That one night of her life when she felt just perfect, the dress that she wore had killed her.

REAL WEIRD

BAD HAIR DAYS

Hair. Long or short, natural or dyed, we all have it. (Well, almost all - maybe a few teachers lack a bit on top!). Some days, no matter what we do with our hair, it just doesn't seem to look or fall right at all. And when we know our hair doesn't look right, we just don't feel right, and nothing seems to go right. *Bad hair days,* these are known as.

Our hair might cause us all sorts of problems throughout our lives, but compare yourself to some of the odd 'hairy' people from the past and you'll perhaps see how trivial your own hair-problems are. Children born covered with hair; hair that turns white from a fright; full heads of hair that drop out from shock and, of course, hairy women with beards, are just some of the actual 'hair facts' of history.

In the C19th, when touring 'Freak Shows' were a popular form of normal entertainment, there were numerous 'hairy' fairground attractions. One of these was known as 'Jo-Jo the Dog Faced Boy'. Jo-Jo was said to resemble a Skye terrier because of the bushy yellow hair that covered his entire face and moustached in long strands from either side of his furry nose. A popular and profitable touring attraction, Jo-Jo was said to have been captured as a 'wild dog-child' in the forests of eastern Europe. Abandoned by his natural parents as a hairy curse, he was claimed to have grown up amongst wolves, feeding upon berries and small animals that he hunted and ate raw. His freak-show act involved scampering around on all fours, snapping and snarling and cocking his leg, imitating the wild dogs that he allegedly resembled. There is no record of what happened to Jo-Jo once he grew up. Perhaps he just shaved like most men do - only cheeks, ears, nose, and all!

One of the most popular attractions at any decent freak-show was always 'The Bearded Lady'. In the 1880's, Janice Deveree, the famous 'Bearded Lady of Kentucky', earned a vast fortune by exhibiting herself with a 35cm beard. Janice travelled widely throughout Europe and America. She lived a life of extreme luxury, and always had a group of adoring men in tow, all who were captivated by her unique looks and charming personality.

Another 'hairy lady' who made a fortune out of her 'gift' was Madame Fortune Clofullia. She had many wealthy lovers, including members of royal families. She was showered with presents of gold and jewels by her lover, the French Emperor Napoleon III, who found her well groomed beard and side-whiskers irresistible. Not content with being loved by royalty, Madame Fortune also joined a touring freak-show. In the USA she made well over 1 million dollars simply by displaying her unconventional features to 3 million people in a single year. She eventually got married, as most bearded ladies did - they seemed to have had no trouble attracting men. She had two children, and at birth her second child, a son, was covered with hair. Even as a baby he had a wispy tuft of a beard. By the time he was four years old, under the stage name 'The Infant Esau', Madame Fortune's son was touring the freak-shows alongside her. Until about the age of thirteen, Esau toured wearing frilly dresses. He was advertised at the shows as 'The Hairy Girl' - and the people willingly paid their money to gawp at 'him'.

Too frizzy, too curly, too greasy, too straight - if your hair is causing you a problem, don't worry about it. Take a lesson from the past, and let your 'problem' become your best feature. Who knows, you might end up making a fortune out of it. And if things come 'on top' you can always shave it all off and go for the ever-trendy, totally bald look.

LONDON UNDERGROUND

Deep beneath the streets and buildings of London, somewhere in the labyrinth of old railway and sewerage tunnels that criss-cross the city, a lost tribe of human beings are said to exist. This race of humans - humans, but barely people - have mutated and adapted to survive in their dark underworld. Allegedly, there are three classes of people who live in the hidden world beneath the city. Lowest in this social order are the unemployed homeless who have retreated from the harsh 'real' world above to a safer, dryer place. These inhabit the higher railway tunnels, and interact between the lower and upper worlds. Many of them are enslaved by the class known as 'Gollums', and often emerge to go begging or shopping for these 'masters' who own them.

Next in the social order come 'The Subway Sect'. These claim to be a highly organised tribe of hippies, punks and New Age Travellers who have completely retreated from the world above. They now exist in a network of underground bunkers, tapping into the water, lighting, TV and Wi-Fi systems from above for free. They survive on food and drink that they steal, or 'liberate', from the cities restaurants and hotel kitchens, into which they have ingeniously burrowed secret entrances.

Finally, there are the 'Gollums', the true kings and masters of this strange underworld.

Gollums are subterranean troglodytes, born and bred in the caves and chasms far below the surface of this world. They rarely come to the surface of the city, and are thought to be an evolved - or rather devolved - breed of humans. Although secretive, hairless and stunted, with slits of eyes that cannot tolerate any daylight, Gollums have immense brain power. Said to be psychic, they are able to control weak human minds by thought-power alone. This strange species is carnivorous. It is believed that even Gollum 'children' will eat flesh raw, as well as drink fresh blood - and they are quite willing for that flesh and blood to be human. Some experts claim that the hundreds of people who vanish mysteriously every year in the capital end up in the larders of these foul cannibal creatures. Whole trainloads of people are claimed to have been hijacked by the Gollums in the busy rush- hour, although such atrocious incidents are hushed up by the authorities. These 'accidents' are not officially recorded for fear that people will stop using the underground rail system.

Although it is well known that their staple diet is actually fresh rat-flesh, Gollums are known to 'farm' and 'herd' humans from the surface, along with dogs, cats and the legendary London sewer-pigs. Gollums are presumed to have evolved from a small group of humans who fled below the surface of the city hundreds of years ago - people fleeing the plagues of the Middle Ages; people who had been branded as 'witches' or 'criminals' in times past; people who did not want to be burned, tortured, or thrown into dungeons. Feeding on whatever they could find, these 'refugees' adapted and survived in the damp underground darkness. Some historians claim that actual Gollum numbers increased after a historical episode which provided them with an unexpected food surplus - the Blitz during the Second World War. In the bombing of London in air-raids, thousands of surface people sought nightly refuge in the railway stations and tunnels. Hundreds of these people disappeared, were never accounted for, and were not recorded as official 'war dead'. Several gnawed skeletons were found in the tunnels at the time, but were declared by the authorities to have been devoured by starving rat swarms.

Always trying to remain quiet and hidden, the Gollums have apparently almost lost the power of speech. They are said to communicate in lisping whispers, or even just by psychic thoughts alone. Nowadays, they prowl the sewers and rail tunnels of the capital, showing themselves as little as possible, and then only to those they know they can control - or will eat!

Several well known writers of have used the Gollums and their underground kingdom in works of fiction, including Raymond Briggs in *Fungus The Bogeyman*, and JRR Tolkien in *Lord Of The Rings*. It is generally thought that Tolkien, in his greatest work, *The Hobbit,* based his evil character 'Gollum' on an encounter he had with one of the real London Gollums while travelling across the city on The Underground.

The last recorded sighting of a real Gollum was in April 2011, when police arrested one of the mysterious creatures for attempting to derail a train at Pimlico underground station. The creature, disguised as a clerical worker in a grey suit, hat and winter coat, is reported to have screeched in agony when brought up to the city's surface. It died of shock at the exposure to bright surface daylight. No identity was found on the sparsely clad body of the Gollum, which was reported as being hideously ugly, something like a cross between a human being and a gigantic mole. The incident is still being investigated by the police.

SLEEPERS

A recent survey for a British medical magazine found that 90 percent of teenagers have trouble getting up in the morning for school. The report in **Medicine Now** claimed that on average, teenagers should sleep for at least nine hours a night. Most young people, the survey claimed, could actually benefit from being allowed at least one extra hour of sleep per night at such a critical stage of the body's development. Most people have days when waking and getting up is difficult. Usually though, they manage to struggle up and rush madly around, hoping that they are not too late for school or work. But what if one morning you simply could not be woken up? What if you slept on and on.... and on?

Snow White. Sleeping Beauty. Rip Van Winkle. Most of us have heard of these fairytale figures who fell into a long sleep from which they could not be roused until years later - and then by a magic kiss, or to find themselves thinking that it was just the next day. Fewer of us realise that a prolonged sleeping state is not just the stuff of fairytales.

There are many real life accounts of people who have suffered from an actual medical condition known as *Prolonged Sleeping Disorder*. PSD is a sleep from which people cannot wake - a condition different from a coma, in which usually some kind of injury has been sustained.

Beliefs about magically-induced sleep have been recorded in many cultures all over the world. In Christian legend the most famous 'sleepers' were *'the seven youths of Ephesus'*. In 250 AD, in Greece, while fleeing from attackers who wanted to kill them for their religious beliefs, these youths hid themselves deep in a mountain cave. After long hours of prayer for salvation, and shocked by their ordeal, all seven youths fell into a deep sleep. Their attackers never found them, and they did not return home. Eventually, the youths were all discovered still sleeping, and still youthful - 200 years later! Even more surprising, they were woken up by the touch of the child who discovered them in their slumber. The seven youths left the cave, thinking that they were returning home to their families and not expecting to find a world that had changed beyond recognition. The miraculous re-awakening of the youths of Ephesus is still celebrated every July 27th in Eastern Christian churches.

Another ancient legend is that of *Epimenides*, who wandered into a nymph-haunted cavern on the island of Crete in the seventh century BC. There in the cave he was lulled into a sleep by the enchanted singing of the beautiful nymphs - a lovely, deep and dreamless sleep that seemed to go on forever. Epimenides woke up over a hundred years later. Thinking that it was simply the next day, and that he might be in trouble with his wife for having stayed out all night, he wandered back down to his home village, there to find himself among complete strangers rather than the family and friends he had left 'the day before'.

In 'real life' rather than legends, the longest recorded human sleep is of an incredible 32 years. On February 22nd 1876, a fourteen year old girl called *Carolina Olsson*, from Monsterns, Sweden, fell into a deep, mysterious, trance-like sleep. The Swedish girl was not injured in anyway, nor had she suffered any violent shock. Carolina woke up on April 3rd, 1908 - 32 years and 42 days later! Although by now she was 46 years old, she looked like a young woman of 25. During her sleep she had barely aged. Her hair and nails had not grown any longer. Most remarkably, she did not suffer any prolonged after-effects from her years of slumber. A few months after her awakening, once she had learned to walk again, she returned to a normal life. Carolina lived on for a further 42 years, dying in 1950, at the grand old age of 89. The cause of her mid-life 'nap' remains a medical mystery

Another sleeping woman, Margaret Boyenval - also

known as *'The Sleeping Woman of Thenolles'* - slept for 20 years between 1883 and 1903. A well known thief, she collapsed into a mysterious sleep after showing signs of distress while expecting a visit to her house by the police. Although otherwise healthy, she slept on despite repeated attempts to rouse her. She was put to bed and left there, with the futile attempts at waking her up by repeatedly slapping and nipping her stopping after the first few months. In 1902, her doctor saw signs of returning consciousness. Margaret opened her eyes, said, 'You're pinching me again!' She then fell back to sleep, and died in her slumber five months later.

In more brutal times past, every attempt would be made to wake the sleeper, including whipping, beating, burning with candle flames, pricking with pins, and the application of hot oils to the body.

So, the next time you fancy a lie-in, or just feel that you need a few hours more sleep, you could always argue that you are just following the recommended advice of a recent medical survey. You could claim that are not just sleeping in, but are actually suffering from a recognised medical condition. You could even just lie there and ignore everybody, keeping your eyes closed while people shout and shake you. But then again, think of what lengths the people you know might go to try and wake you up - would you put it past them to try flames, pins or the application of hot oils? Maybe you should just get up though, and seize the day. *Carpe diem!* After all, you can sleep when you're dead. And, as the saying goes, 'You're a long time dead'.

TOXIC SLUDGE MUTANTS

When the sludge pits at Delphi Motor Systems Plant in Anderson, Indiana, USA, were cleaned out last November, workers made a bizarre discovery. They found a colony of what one 30 year old employee described as 'squid like creatures'. The creatures were the colour of earthworms, 20cm long, with seven tentacles, head-spines, and several eyes. The pit, which contained anti-freeze, paint stripper, oil and various acids - a chemical cocktail used in the formation of plastic car bumpers - held several of the creatures. One of the 'squidgers' was taken out, killed, and placed in a specimen jar. It was displayed in the work area for several days before being stolen in early December.

Scientists from the local Nabrasksa University examined the pit and others nearby. On March 4th, both the US Environmental Protection Agency and the university confirmed that 'a reptilian creature of unknown origin or type' had been found in the sludge pit. Tamara Ohl, spokeswoman for the EPA, said that Delphi Motors had promised that if they found another sample of the organism, they would preserve it alive and send it for testing.

... AND MUTANT FROGS

Deformed frogs were first reported in Minnesota, USA, on 8 August 2012 by school students from Le Seur, after a school field trip to local wetlands. Of the 22 frogs caught by pupils that day, 11 were mutants. Since then more frogs with grotesquely deformed or extra limbs, spiral tails, missing eyes and even short horns have been found in 54 of Minnesota's 87 counties. Other mutant frogs have turned up in neighbouring Wisconsin and South Dakota, and even as far away as Quebec.

Theories to try and explain the deformities include pesticides used by local farmers; mutant skin parasites which effect the development of young frogs; acid rain and radiation exposure due to the damaged ozone layer. The suitably named Doctor David Hoppet, a herpetologist from the University of Minnesota, stated: 'These new abnormalities are widespread. This shows that the problem has more than one source. My own research suggests water pollution, caused by something airborne, such as heavy metals like lead or mercury. These could be coming from local motor manufacturing plants. I must stress, this is a 'best guess'. These deformities coincide with an overall global decline in numbers of frogs, toads and salamanders. We must never forget that this planet is a fragile place.'

Another expert, Doctor Miriam Leezard, blamed the problem firmly on a group of French genetic engineers. She claimed that, in France, scientists were attempting to breed frogs with extra legs to help combat a shortage of the French delicacy in restaurants and supermarkets. Mutant genes had somehow been bred into the general amphibian population, with deformed frogs being the result. French scientists have strenuously denied this and claimed ridiculous comic stereotypes are behind the absurd accusation. They confirmed that none of their six legged, kitchen-bound frogs had escaped from the laboratories.

More mutant frogs turned up in a city park in Kitakyushu, Fukuoka, Japan, last October. Fifty nine frogs of a species known as Yamaakagaeru that were captured by children had extra legs, 3 extra eyes, and claws on the ends of their webbed feet. More worrying, the frogs were developing land-based predatory habits, hunting and feeding on mice, squirrels and other small rodents.

Environmental experts report that frogs, with their sensitive skins and a life cycle that is both aquatic and land-based, are often key indicators of the environment's health. With the increased incidence of mutant frogs being reported world-wide, it would seem that the planet is indeed a fragile place, and that we all have good reason to worry.

WORLD WIDE MYTHS

THE SWAN CHILDREN OF LIR - Irish

In Ireland there once lived a god known as Lir, The Father of the Sea. Lir married two sisters. The first sister, who died in an accident, left him four children - a girl named Fionuala and three younger boys called Aod, Conn and Fiachra. The second sister, Aoife, remained childless, and acted as a mother to her sister's children. These children loved their father and followed him around like a pack of puppy dogs. There was never a moment's peace with them, and this fact, along with Lir's devoted love for his yapping children, made their stepmother-aunt intensely jealous. As any reader of tales will know, there is little worse for a pack of royal children than a jealous stepmother. True to form, after a busy day of runny noses, cut knees and bedtime tears, Aoife swore that she could tolerate the children no longer, and she decided to get rid of them, in the cruellest way.

With murder in mind, she set off on a journey across the mountains to visit her brother, Bov The Red, who was also a god-king. She took the four children along with her as a holiday treat. The journey led them past a remote and wild place along the shore of Lough Derravaragh, a great lake in the heart of Ireland. Here Aoife ordered her servants to cut the throats of the children then throw their bodies into the lake. Fearing the anger of King Lir more than the cruelty of Aoife, the servants refused to kill the children. They tried to run away along the lake shore, but before they had got very far Aoife used her magical powers to turn the lot of them into standing stones. To this day The Servants Of Lir can be found scattered as stone pillars along the shores of the Lough. Aoife now turned upon the terrified children. She drew out her dagger, but could not find it in her heart to butcher them herself. Instead of killing them, she muttered more magical charms which transformed all four children into white swans. In her enchantments Aoife placed the following curse upon the swan children:

'Three hundred years you'll spend by the gentle waters of this lake; three hundred years in bitter cold you'll waste upon the Giant's Causeway; three hundred years be blasted by the Atlantic winds around Galway Bay. After that, only when The Man of The North is married to The Bride of The South will this curse be lifted.'

Aoife went on with her journey, but using magic for evil had drained her of all power and beauty. Bov the Red, shocked at the sight of his withered sister, questioned her about the missing children, and she confessed to her crime. Fearing what Lir would do his sister, Bov turned her into a 'demon of the air'. She flew away shrieking like a seagull, and played no part in the tale, but can still be heard moaning and wailing around the mountains of the Ring of Kerry in the far south west of Ireland.

Lir received news of what had happened to his children. He looked for them in the lakes and mountains, and eventually found them gliding upon the surface of the lake. They were overjoyed to see their father again, and greeted him with beautiful songs. They still had the power of human speech, and now also the gift of song and wonderful music. From all parts of Ireland people gathered on the lake shore to hear the beautiful singing, and to converse with the amazing swans.

After three hundred years as swans, all enjoyment in their song had gone. The music was not frequent, and rarely so sweet. The swans, following the lay of Aoife's curse, flew north, taking up the next stage of their life by the wild cliffs and angry seas of the northern coast. The nights were bitter and frosty. Fionuala, the eldest swan-child, mothered her younger brothers, wrapping her wings around them, trying to keep out the worst of the frost. Like this, they endured three hundred years of torment until the next stage of the curse was upon them. They took flight to the western cliffs, and here too they suffered much hardship and endured hard times. Still, they often sang sweetly – music was their only comfort in the darkest of their days

When the final phase of their suffering was upon them, the swans decided to fly south to the palace of their father, Lir, who had long ago passed from this earth. They arrived at their old home, but were shocked and bewildered to find nothing but green barrows and ruined mounds where once their own palace had stood. At Erris Bay, so the legend goes, the children heard the sound of a Christian bell for the first time. They were frightened by the thin, metallic sound, but fascinated also, for it was a new kind of music to them. The bell was ringing out from the chapel on an old hermit who had settled on the bay to worship his god. The four swans lined up beside him, and when he stopped his praying they promptly asked him what all the noise was about. Thinking that the talking swans were angels sent from Heaven, the hermit took them in as his guests.

It so happened that a princess of the area, Deoca, 'the beauty of the south', was due to marry a northern king. They were very much in love, and wanted to have the most spectacular wedding the country had ever seen. At the couple's request, the hermit took the singing swan-children along to their wedding so that everyone there could hear the beautiful singing of the 'birds'. The swan children arrived at the moment the two lovers were joined in marriage by the Christian priest. Now, the final part of Aoife's curse fell upon them, for man of the North and the bride of the South were married together at last. The plumage of the swans fell away. Their wings dropped off to reveal human arms. Soon, standing before the astonished crowd, were the four young children of King Lir. But in this miracle, Time had finally caught up with them. Before the gathering the smiling children aged and withered a thousand years within a matter of seconds. The centuries took their toll, until at last there was nothing of the children but four piles of golden dust upon the chapel floor. A gentle wind came blowing through the hall and the dust was gathered up in spinning cloud, with beautiful music spilling from the golden cloud as it was blown westward toward the horizon. At last, the curse was lifted. The swan-children's souls were at peace. Their tale was at its end, although here it is told once more so that it can pass on still into the future.

THE BIRTH OF GARUDA - A Hindu Myth

Kasyapa was a wise old man who had two beautiful wives, Kadru and Vinata. Both were the daughters of ancient gods, and much was expected of any children that they might have. Because they had magical powers, Kadru and Vinata could choose the number and appearance of their first born children. One day Kasyapa went to his wives in turn and told them that it was time to decide upon the fate of their children. Kadru, who wanted to protect the secrets of Heaven from men, chose to have a thousand serpents for her first sons. She asked that each one would be strong, as well as splendid to look upon. Her sister Vinata wanted only two sons. Her wish was that in their strength, grace, beauty and wisdom her twins would be superior to any of Kadru's thousand serpent-sons. Her twins, she wished, would one day be able to present men with all the secrets of Heaven that her sister wanted to protect. In his wisdom, Kasyapa granted both his wives their wishes, then he withdrew into the silence and solitude of a forest, warning the women that they should take great care to protect his unborn children.

Nine hundred Earth-years passed, then Kadru laid a thousand tiny eggs. Three more years went by, then Vinata gave birth to two large red eggs. The sisters clucked and fussed over their fragile creations like two birds, and indeed both made great nests in the heart of the Earth where they could keep their eggs safe, dry and warm. After five hundred years of incubation the thousand serpent sons of Kadru broke out of their shells and swarmed about their delighted mother. Vinata looked on, longing to see her own sons in the world, but her twins did not appear, not even after a further three years.

Vinata watched her sister's sons grow stronger, leave their mother's nest and spread over the earth. Growing jealous and impatient, she eventually went to her nest and broke open one of the eggs to see what was happening. Inside she found a human embryo but with only the upper half developed, the lower half still being a serpent's tail with the sprouting feet of a bird. This half-formed child, whose skin flickered like living starlight and danced like moonlit flames, opened his dazzling eyes. When he saw that he was brought too soon into the world he began to weep tears of molten gold. He was called Aruna - the red glow of dawn. Cursing his foolish and impatient mother, he began to fly up from the heart of darkness toward the dark sky beyond the opening of his nest-cave. As he flew, he sang a beautiful song which predicted a wonderful future for his unborn brother. His song also told of a future war between the humans and the serpents which lived upon the surface of the Earth. Aruna rose up into the sky, where he has remained ever since, leading the red chariot which hauls up the sun each new day.

Another three hundred years passed, and although still impatient, the sight of her first son's face every morning reminded Vinata not to be hasty or foolish. She just sat by her nest and waited. One morning a scratching came from within the egg. It broke open, and out stepped her second son, fully grown, and truly beautiful. This was Garuda, who was destined to become known as 'The Eater Of All Serpents'. His skin was pale blue, his fierce eyes as bright and yellow as midday sunshine, and above his arms he had the glorious wings of a golden eagle. The thousand serpent children of Kadru gathered from all corners of the world to look upon him, and for the first time in their short lives they trembled, and knew fear. He seemed to shimmer and change form beneath their gaze. One moment he was a beautiful youth, the next a winged elephant with the beak and talons of an eagle, the next he was a dazzling cloud of mist that could not be penetrated by sight, or by weapon. Before the sight of Garuda the serpent children fled to their hundred palaces and city grottos that they had built beneath the earth and in the clouds. Here they gathered up treasures that they stole from the gods and men, and hoarded all manner of weapons with which to protect their wealth. Waiting for their cousin to emerge from his underground nest, they enslaved humans and animals to form great armies, preparing themselves for the day when they would have to protect themselves from Garuda, Eater Of All Serpents.

KING PERUN THE TONGUELESS – Europe

Why should you touch every round, white pebble? This tale will tell you :-

Perun The Tongueless, king of the northern lands, was a great wizard who only ever used his power for good. He invited wizards, witches, warlocks and magicians from all over the world to his palace. He used magic wisely, healing sick people, making the land fertile and keeping dangerous animals away from the country. To entertain his children he would turn a stone into a bird, make snow fall from the ceiling, or vanish away in a puff of smoke.

Only one wizard in the world refused to visit Perun. He was called Darkness and lived in the forests of the east. Darkness was an evil wizard. He hated the idea of visiting a king who used magic wisely and for the good. Perun decided to visit Darkness in the hope of becoming his friend. Alone, on a white horse, he travelled east in search of the palace of Darkness. After several weeks he came to the edge of an oak forest. There was not a bird or animal to be seen; the place was all shadow and silence. The white horse was afraid and would not enter the forest. Perun released it, and continued his way on foot. After many hours of quiet walking he heard laughter and voices through the trees. He stepped into a clearing, but it was empty. A wind came howling through the forest, the sky above went black and flashed with lightning. Then from behind the trees around the clearing stepped giant trolls, dozens of them, all with yellow eyes and gleaming white fangs. They were the servants of the evil wizard, Darkness.

'Who are you that dares come into the forest owned by Darkness?' a troll demanded. But of course Perun, having no tongue, could not answer.

'Tell us your name and your business,' the troll shouted. When he did not answer again, the trolls were on him in a second, and they tied him to a great tree. In a clap of thunder, wizard Darkness appeared in the clearing. He was as tall as a tree, with black hair, black eyes and skin as white as clouds. When Darkness saw that the captured stranger had no tongue he knew immediately who it was.

'So, it's good King Perun, fastened to a tree in a forest, so far away from home,' he hissed.

'Well, Perun, I've heard you are something of a wizard. And they say you have a heart of gold. Let's see if that's true, shall we.'

Darkness ordered his trolls to cut out Perun's heart. Perun knew that to escape he would have to use the power of magic. When the trolls approached him with their knives he turned into a small white mouse. The ropes no longer held him to the tree and he scampered away into the forest. But Darkness turned himself into a black cat and went chasing after the mouse. Perun changed from a mouse into a dog. He turned round, barking, and chased the cat. Darkness transformed from a cat into a bear. He turned round, growling, and went after the dog. Perun became a tiger, turned around, snarling, and ran at the bear. But Darkness was a powerful wizard. He waited until Perun sprang forward toward him. Just as the bear was about to be landed on by the tiger, the bear changed into the animal that all other animals, including man, fear and despise most - a deadly, black serpent. The black snake coiled, fangs bared, ready to strike the tiger. Perun knew that if the serpent bit him, he would die. Using all the power he could muster he managed to turn from a springing tiger into a white dove, wings flapping, flying upwards, the serpent's fangs just scraping at his tail feathers. He flew hard, high into the sky, relieved to have escaped from the evil wizard and his trolls.

Perun decided to try and fly around the world and back to his home in the north. When he was over the middle of the ocean he noticed a tiny speck high above him. The speck came closer, growing larger, moving faster. It was Darkness, now in the form of an eagle. Perun, still a dove, flew down toward the water. The eagle was getting closer and closer. Perun transformed into a fish and dropped into the waters of the ocean. The moment he hit the water he turned himself into a small, white pebble and sank quickly to the bottom of the sea. Darkness had not seen Perun turn into a pebble. Thinking that the king was still a fish, he turned into a shark and dived into the ocean. The sea was full of small fish. Darkness went chasing after every little fish in the ocean, looking for the one that was Perun, but of course he could find nothing of him. Perun The Tongueless, in the shape of a small pebble, was resting at the bottom of the deep green ocean. In escaping Darkness, he had exhausted himself, and did not have the power to change back from a stone into a human being.

For countless years Perun has lain at the bottom of the ocean in the cold, black world of stones. The waves have pushed him eastwards, the currents dragged him north. He can do nothing but lie there, feeling ice cold and seeing nothing, wondering if he would ever get back to his home and children. He is there to this day, waiting for the mercy of the gods, or the touch of a human hand. These, so it is said, are the only things that can release him from his terrible pebble-prison.

WWF MINOTAUR – Ancient Greece

Welcome this afternoon to the island of Crete and the royal palace of King Minos, where we hope to bring you live fight action from the spectacular Labyrinth here. Theseus, the young Greek warrior and the poor underdog in this challenge, meets the legendary Minotaur. Yes folks, *that* Minotaur - half man, half bull. The Warrior and the Bull Beast are in the Labyrinth as we speak, searching each other out in the darkness. There's Theseus in view now, wandering around with a ball of string, sword already in his hand. It's expected to be a brutal fight - no holds barred, anything goes. A typical Greek death-match, though I can't say looking at Theseus that I fancy his chances. Well, as you see up above ground it's glorious weather - the blue Mediterranean sea and blue sky, lovely sunshine, lovely views. There's a little crowd of spectators gathered around the Labyrinth entrance, amongst them the sacrificial youths from Greece who face certain death unless Theseus can kill the Minotaur. There's old Daedalus who designed the labyrinth, along with his son Icarus. And there, biting her nails, is a very anxious looking local lady, a certain Princess Ariadne, who according to the local gossip has just become engaged to Theseus. Well, this afternoon's grudge fight might prove theirs to be one of the shortest love affairs in history. Let's hope not though - as the saying goes, only time will tell. Theseus may well be the underdog, but he's seen plenty of battle action all around the world, and as you know, on the day anything can happen.

And now we return you underground to the Labyrinth. Theseus has just stepped into the torchlit chamber where the Minotaur is already waiting. The match is on. It's moments away now. Theseus puts down his ball of thread. The Minotaur - look at him! Great gods! What a beast. He's just glaring at Theseus, pawing at the ground with his front hoof. Three hundred pounds of hair, horn and muscle. He's snorting and bellowing, ready to charge. Theseus looks positively puny here now. So, a frail looking Theseus, sword ready, looking confident despite the size difference. Checks the dagger that's strapped to his leg. He bows politely, a true martial artist. And they're off. Here we go, Minotaur versus Theseus. Minotaur charging forward, tries to skewer Theseus on those cruel, razor-sharp horns. Trying to kebab him, Greek style. Theseus side - stepping, swiping wildly across with his sword - the clank of metal sword on solid bull horn. Uncomfortably close that for the Minotaur, who deflects another wild sideswipe and is in... pushing forward, forcing poor Theseus back now. Theseus, driven back against the rock wall. He's pinned up. One twist of horn now, and he's bull-meat. He drops, rolling to the left - and would you believe that! Theseus escapes. He's taken a scrape on the shoulder though, and there's blood, but he's back on his feet. He's crouched, ready for more action, sword firm and steady out front. The Minotaur looks confused. He's not used to his opponents getting out of that one. They're circling each other now, the Minotaur wary. Coming forward. Theseus springs forward, jabs up - oh, and he's nicked him. He's caught the Minotaur's ribs with a sneaky uppercut. There's blood. The beast is bellowing. He's looking down at his chest in amazement and just can't believe he's been cut. Look at him, he's furious - you might say he's seeing red. His horns are slashing this way and that, up and down, Theseus weaving away, dodging. He's quick - he's lightning quick. But oh no, look at that! Kebab time. The Greek's taken a horn full in the shoulder. His sword's dropped, clattering to the floor. It's close combat now, Theseus desperately grabbing onto the left horn, trying to stop it pushing further into his shoulder. The Minotaur is swinging him wildly, trying to smash him against the rocks, but this Greek kid is not letting go. And down they go, rolling on the floor, grappling in dust, sweat and blood. I'd put my money on the Minotaur in this position - he must weigh at least three times more than the Greek - he must be favourite now. But look at that! Oh, that was dirty! Theseus butted him. A full head-butt right on the nose. The Bull-beast is screaming in rage. That was nasty. That was dirty. But in this game, the only rules are no rules. Anything goes. And Theseus wastes no time. He's up with a dagger. Minotaur trying to back away. Theseus jabs straight through the centre and into the chest. Oh... it's there.... it's there. The dagger's in the bull-beast's chest. Surely, that's it now. The Minotaur can't survive that. Listen to those squeals of pain. Listen - the crowd outside are cheering like mad - they think it's all over. Down goes the Minotaur, on his knees. Theseus, bloody Theseus - he's covered in the stuff. He's standing there, rubbing at his injured shoulder. He knows he's got it won. He's taking up his sword now. He's testing the blade on his thumb. It wouldn't surprise me if he's going to take the bull's head off. Next stop, butcher's shop for the Minotaur, whose gone down onto his face. He's not even moving. Barely a twitch. Theseus raises his sword high above his head. Surely, it's all over now...

WEIRD TALES

WONDERMITES

Dennis, my dad's mate's stepson, first alerted us to the Wondermite menace. Not tiny little dust mites, those microscopic creatures that live in your carpets and beds and even on your clothes - everyone knows about those. Dennis told us about the strange and special mites. He used to work as a lab technician at Virotex, that place where they engineer special viruses to kill off crop pests and animal diseases. It's a hi-tech laboratory in Ipswich that looks as though it should be on Mars, and the whole place is full of mad scientists. Some of the work they do there is top secret, dangerous stuff. Dad says he's amazed that Dennis ever got a job there, not because he's seventeen and spotty, but because he's as clumsy as a hippo in a bottle shop, and doesn't know a thing about science. He can't even boil water properly.

At one of the labs in Virotex they were working with dust mites. If you suffer from asthma or eczema like me, you'll know that some experts blame dust mites for causing the itching and breathing problems that can come with these. Well, not the mites exactly, but what they produce - their waste deposits. Their excrement! Too horrible to think about, really. They feed on human tissue and dead skin, the bits of us that drop off into our beds, settees and carpets - the stuff that we call dust. The scientists at Virotex were trying to create a new type of mite that could not digest this skin. They were tinkering around with genes to make a fast breeder that would be introduced to carpets and beds all over the world. Dust mite babies would be born that could no longer digest the dust. Thus, the super-breeders would gradually breed themselves into extinction, with dust mites world-wide starving to death in about a year. That was the theory, anyway.

The trouble with this cunning plan was that Dennis worked there at Virotex. Wiping the lab top one Friday morning, he knocked a rack of test-tubes over and spilled some of the contents. Nobody was about, so he quickly topped them up from an un-spilled tube, then added bit of tap water, hoping that no one would ever notice the difference. After the weekend, when Dennis arrived back at work, all the scientists were running about in a panic, waving their arms and babbling. In one of the mite-tanks something strange had happened - the dust mites had started growing. Each generation was slightly bigger than the last, each new dust mite 'child' growing bigger than its parents. This had not been expected or predicted. One scientist let Dennis have a look at a new Wondermite through an electron microscope - it was a hideous, hairy, furry, spidery looking thing. The scientist told Dennis that if this new type of Dermathophagoides (dust mites to you and me) carried on breeding and growing at their present rate, they would be visible to the naked eye in about a fortnight.

One of Dennis's duties at Virotex had been to feed the dust mites. Each morning he had to sprinkle them with fresh dust from a little pepper pot. But he was not now allowed to look after the new Wondermites, which were considered too important for non-specialist feeding. A senior laboratory technician was put in charge of them, a real old miser who was really mean with the dust-pot. Dennis was sure he wasn't giving the new mites enough dust. Whenever the lab was quiet he would slide off the mite-tank lid and give them an extra sprinkle, or even toss in a few crumbs and scraps left over from his ham sandwiches.

One afternoon, while Dennis was secretly feeding the Wondermites, the door of the lab swung open and the senior technician marched in. Dennis ducked down out of sight before sneaking away through the mite-tanks. In his haste, he left the lid of the tank open a crack. The tank was open all that day and all night - needless to say, most of the Wondermites escaped. When Virotex found the lid open and their mites gone, Dennis owned up.

Despite his heroic honesty, he was sacked. The whole Wondermite story was quickly hushed up, and the newspapers never got to hear about them at the time. But now, of course, they're onto it, and Ipswich is crawling with journalists. Too many things have happened, and Dennis reckons that his story is worth tens of thousands of pounds to the newspapers.

The bad things started in Holywells Park. Dogs began to go missing while retrieving sticks from the long grass. Old people who went for pleasant strolls in the Botanical Gardens never returned. Naughty children who played out too late at night mysteriously disappeared. Then the police began to find skeletons - human skeletons - picked clean, not a scrap of flesh or skin left on them. A month or so later, when the sightings of mice-sized mites began, Virotex could no longer cover up the story. Their Wondermites had escaped, were breeding like mad rabbits, and they were no longer interested in eating just dead skin. It seemed that somewhere along the line they had acquired a taste for meat - a predilection for fresh flesh. The fresher the better, it seemed. A cat, a dog, a pig, a human; basically, they would eat anything that moved.

The military cordoned off the park, then went in with guns and flame throwers blazing. The mites were quicker than frightened rats, and most of them managed to escape down into the sewers. They're all over the city now, and not just underground. They seem to prefer living in fields, hedgerows and grass verges - any kind of vegetation that reminds them of human beds or hairy carpets.

Our next door neighbour says that she was attacked by the mites, but luckily escaped with just a few bites on the legs. She says that they hunt in packs. There you are, walking along past a field or some shrubbery, minding your own quiet business, when suddenly you hear a rustling and rattling in the grass beside you. Next thing, a dozen giant mites with fat, round bodies and spiny legs are leaping out and giving chase, legs clickering, beakish jaws snapping away.

Now, the mites are the size of dogs. The scientists say that if they carry on breeding and feeding at the present rate, in two years time they will be as big as cows.

Personally, I didn't believe any of the Wondermite stories at first, not even the TV and newspaper reports. I didn't believe Dennis, or our next door neighbour - not until I was down watching the football at Portman Road. You might have seen it yourself, Ipswich versus Norwich, live on Sky

Sport just the other week - it made all the news channels. It's there on Youtube. Just before half time a pack of about twenty giant mites emerged from a tunnel beneath the pitch and started chasing the players and referee. They were huge, easily the size of dogs, and there they were, on the pitch, on live TV, for all the world to see! I just couldn't believe it when the referee went down screaming under a scrum of them. The worst thing, though, was that the crowd started cheering! Well, nobody likes a referee, do they?

THE INCREDIBLE EXPANDING REPTILE

Tom connected the air tube of dad's old foot-pump to a drinking straw, and the trap was almost ready. All that it needed now was baiting. Louise's nosy nature would take care of that. She was such a little brat. He knew that she would not be able to resist asking questions about the reptile. Tom slid open the garage door and watched his horrible little sister skipping to a chanted rhyme in the garden:

> *'Big brown bread crumbs*
> *By the pricking of my thumbs*
> *Something wicked this way comes...'*

Tom slouched against the front of the open garage. His hand clasped 'The Incredible Expandable Reptile', bought in secret at a sea-side joke-shop on their last holiday. At a glance the toy looked alive, and Tom had been practicing his puppetry skills. He peered down at the toy, muttering as though it was real, 'Oh, does he want feeding then? Lovely creature... little cutesy.' As he had predicted, the skipping and rhyme jerked to a halt. Louise came edging toward the garage doorway.

'What do you have there, Tommy?'
'Nothing.' Tom grinned. The trap was set.

Earlier that day Louise had landed her brother in

trouble again. This time she had told their mum that he was using the garage as a den. The garage had been strictly out of bounds since dad had left home, and Tom had been punished - he had been made to clean the bath, and toilet! But now it was Sunday afternoon. Mum was busy sorting out the washing and ironing. Tom hoped that revenge would be sweet.

Glancing at Louise, he continued to stroke the plastic reptile, careful to keep it shielded from Louise's view.

'What is it, Tommy?' she tried again.

'Go away,' he snarled, 'or you'll be sorry.'

'Come on, Tommy, let me see it, please.'

'No way - you told mum about the garage. Anyway, it's nothing that would interest you. It's just a creature I found down near the chemical works when I was out frogging.'

'Is that all it is? A silly old frog.'

'No, it's not a frog. Much better.' He held the reptile up toward his face, still keeping it from Louise's view.

'Oh come on Tommy, show me. If you don't, I'll tell mummy you've been in the garage again.'

Tom grinned, eyes narrowing.

'Oh, all right, I'll show you. But not outside - it doesn't like bright daylight. Come in here...'

Louise dropped her skipping rope to the drive and

followed Tom into the garage.

'Come along, to the back,' he said. Louise was a little worried. She sniffed, cringing away from the dusty, cob-webbed walls.

'This better be worth seeing, Tommy.'

He held up the toy, nipping the spines of its neck, making it wriggle and squirm, a pink tongue rasping in and out, so that in the gloom it looked absolutely life-like. Louise gasped, astonished.

'Urgh! What is it? It's horrible. Squash it!"

He laughed, his chuckles echoing from the cluttered walls.

'Don't know what it is. I found two of them in this bog of bubbling mud down near the power station. One's dead now. I blew it up already.'

'It's not a red toad, is it?' Louise whispered, peeping closer. 'Its skin is all baggy and warty like a toad's.'

'No, it's no toad. Look - six legs! Never seen one before, but they blow up even better than frogs. Just watch this...'

Moving to the centre of the garage, he produced a drinking straw from his pocket then inserted it into a hole at the back of the toy. Louise's eyes widened with horror. She was completely fooled, thinking that the creature was real.

'Don't blow it in here Tommy - it'll make an

awful mess! Goo will get everywhere!'

'So what? Mum never comes in here. Now move back against the wall.'

Louise stepped back, anxious to get away from the ugly reptile. She really wanted to get out of the garage, but watching her brother blow up frogs always fascinated her. She really wanted to see what would happen to this new creature. Taking a deep breath, Tom put the straw to his lips and began to blow. Just as the packaging had promised, the 'Incredible Expandable Reptile' inflated easily, like a balloon, and made farty, squeaking sounds. Within a few deep blown breaths it was the size of his head. Louise giggled at the creature's silly noises.

'Oh Tommy, you are just so flipping cruel!'
She shielded her face behind a trembling, raised arm, expecting the creature to pop at any moment. As Tom blew faster the reptile bloated bigger and bigger, the thinning stretchable plastic becoming transparent.

'When it explodes its dirty insides will get everywhere. Mum will hang you, Tommy!'

Tom stopped blowing, rummaged in his pocket then tossed a safety pin to his sister.

'Here - you'll need that.'
She frowned and picked up the pin as Tom backed

toward the garage door. He connected the foot-pump into the creature's straw then began stamping rapidly. Just as advertised, the reptile expanded 'to improbable dimensions'. Within seconds Louise was completely blocked in the back of the garage.

'Tommy!' she shrieked. 'Stop it! Let it go now. Please...'

Her voice was dull and muffled. She shrank right back against the wall as the thing bobbled toward her, the face stretched into a wide, grinning mask. Through the yellow bubble of skin she could just make out the shape of her brother, blocking up the straw-end with his chewing gum. The creature remained inflated. Laughing grimly, Tom stepped from the garage and closed the door. He sauntered across the lawn and slumped beneath the apple tree, smiling as he waited for the inevitable loud 'pop'.

In the dimness of the garage Louise pressed herself back against the dusty wall. She toyed with the safety-pin, pricking at her thumb with the sharp point, trying to pluck up the courage to do what she knew she had to do to make her safe escape.

(author's note – no real reptiles were killed or injured while researching and writing this story!)

THE MAL-BEAST – YORK'S GOLEM

'Twixt a high gate and a low gate
Where Earth meets the Sky
In view of cross and Holy Rose
You'll find Mal-Beast's eye...'

Walking around the ancient and beautiful city of York, looking at the ground from time to time, you might be surprised to notice glass spheres, not unlike eyeballs, fixed randomly into stone paving slabs. Once you've noticed one, you'll notice more. And should you come upon the spot mentioned in the rhyme above, which these days is across the road from a brand name coffee bar, you'll notice that the 'eyeball' there is somewhat different from all the others. For a start, it is blood red. It glows mysteriously, and indeed, seems to follow your every movement, as if staring right up at you maliciously. Crouch down to it – touch it, if you dare. The surface gives beneath your finger – not glass. It gives beneath the finger and has a warm, wobbly feel. It feels like jelly! You have touched the Mal-Beast's eyeball, and are cursed to a future of debt, nasty children and a life of misery.

What is this eyeball? How did it come to be there? When was it set in the middle of the pavement? Well, this is a story rarely told, for it is full of dark deeds and horror, and the good folk of York are somewhat embarrassed by the terrible past doings of their kinsfolk. But we'll tell it here, at the risk of letting slip one of the city's best kept secrets, and putting half the population of York in mortal danger.

*

The story, in a way, is rooted in Prague, one of Europe's most beautiful cities, almost as attractive as York itself. If you're lucky enough to have been there, you'll have heard of the Prague Golem – a terrible, demonic gentile-slaying monster created out of river mud by Rabbi Judah Loew ben Bezabel in the sixteenth century. There was a long history of black arts and necromancy amongst the folk of certain ghettos in Prague, and for many centuries before Bezabel's creation the darker inclined there had been perfecting the art of constructing vile monsters and conjuring up demons. To the city of Prague is where Jazeb Jonahs, a Jew of York, fled after surviving the terrible atrocities committed in York at the castle around Cliffords Tower in the month of March in the year 1190. A rampaging mob, whipped up into a blood-frenzy and led by Richard Malbysse, had attacked property and killed Jews in the city. As the plaque states outside Clifford's Tower, 150 Jews and Jewesses sought sanctuary in the Royal Castle that stood there then. They were ignored by the authorities, and besieged in the castle for a week. Rather than surrender to the blood-thirsty mob, they chose to perish 'at each other's hands'. One hundred and fifty men, women and children killed by each other in ways too dark, gruesome and horrible for us to mention here. One hundred and fifty out of one hundred and fifty one. For there was a single survivor of the atrocity.

Jazeb Jonahs had been a slip of a boy at the time of the pogrom, skinny and small, even for his age. His father, having extinguished the life of Jazeb's mother and siblings in front of his son, deemed that his youngest son was too young to perish in such a terrible way. There was, and in fact still is, a narrow crevice in the tower, high up in the south wall, where by some quirk of design and a lip of stone, it is impossible to notice or see into it from the ground. Into this narrow gap Jazeb's father stuffed the terrified boy with a loaf of bread and a pitcher of water.

'Stay hidden there for as long as you can,' his father had hissed. 'And remember – survive and forgive.' He then slit his own throat and became one of the perished before the boy's very eyes.

His father's final words Jazeb carried with him to the grave. 'Survive and forgive,' he had said. A wise old fool in Jazeb's eyes. Forgive! How he could he forgive? Embittered, twisted by all that he witnessed and heard in the tower that day, he changed the request to a more fitting one of his own: 'Survive and avenge!'

He muttered this day in, day out as he grew up, a refugee who had made his way across Europe after the atrocities.
'Survive and avenge.'
It was on his mind day and night as he trained himself in the Black Arts in the sourest ghettos of Prague; it was his sole reason for surrendering his normal life up to study magic and necromancy under wizened, old magic masters; it was why he eventually mastered the wicked art of summoning up ghouls and demons; it was why he experimented with making monsters out of mud, animal limbs and human body parts which he then sought to animate with the raised spirits of the most bitter and twisted of demons.

Jazeb Jonahs was in his thirty third year when he returned to York as a travelling tailor. He arrived with a horse and cart, upon which, in the centre of his work tools, fabrics and belongings, was a large oak trunk, just about big enough to hold the body of a man. He took lodgings in the ginnels around Coney Street, in the rough quarter, and set up his trade. Though still a Jew, he hid his faith now, and indeed had wandered far from the paths and strict codes and practices of Judaism in his quest for a sorcerer's powers. He was very much an outcast, even from his own people, but he was gifted in his trade, and soon had enough customers to enable his business to flourish. His real business, however, his real 'craft', took place at night when the shops and houses were locked up and when the last lamps and night candles of the neighbourhood had long been extinguished.

Vile rhythmic mutterings, strange chanting, bizarre animal noises and strangled screams might have been heard by his neighbours had they pressed an ear to his wall. And eventually, on the ninth full moon after his return to the city, those ears would have heard another noise – stranger, weirder, more chilling and gruesome than the rest. It was a blood thirsty, whining growl of such a pitch that it instilled horror and terror into those unfortunate enough to hear it. For it came for the creature that Jazeb had called up and constructed and filled with the spirit of one of Hell's most terrible beings. He had made his own golem and animated it with the spark of 'life'. And this golem he named Mal-Beast, translated as Sick Beast, after Malbysse, the leader of the mob who had attacked his kith and kin in the murderous times all those years ago. The Mal-Beast was ravenous, ready to do the work bid by its master. 'Survive and avenge,' Jazeb cackled as he unbolted his dwelling door and let the creature slip out into the night. The Mal-Beast had been given a simple brief for its deeds of horror - find any survivors or blood descendents of those who participated in the deeds at Clifford's Tower, tear open their skulls and feed upon their living brains.

Five victims it took on the streets of York that first night. Ten the second night. Fifteen the third. And then, as the moon waned, the Mal-Beast lost its strength and power. It was returned to its wooden trunk to await the next full moon, when the pattern of bloody revenge could begin again.

After three full moons of carnage – with over a hundred victims dead – the whole of York was gripped with terror. A monster was amongst them, and nobody knew from whence it came, or why. The people were panicking and fleeing the city, and were so stirred up they were but a hair's breadth from rebellion against their overlords. Pressure was on to find the source of the terrible doings and put the city at ease again.

Jazeb's quest for revenge had driven him to the edge of madness. He barely worked as a tailor now, but wandered the streets, glaring at York folk while muttering curses and spitting on the pavement. His eccentric behaviour drew attention to him. He was soon seen as a mad-man, and thus linked to the recent atrocities. He was arrested and dragged down to the cells, and there quickly tortured to see what he might know. The implements of torture in those days, which can be seen today in York Dungeon, were far more effective than dunking a prisoner's head down a toilet or buzzing them with cattle prods, or perhaps depriving them without food and sleep for half a day. Jazeb, up against spikes, the rack, hot irons and raw salted eyes, held out for as long as he could – a full day. With a cruel, bone cracking final stretch on the rack he found himself shrieking and babbling out his terrible quest and secret. After more hours on the stretch-rack he told of his survival of the York Castle pogrom and of the Mal-Beast that lay resting in the oak trunk back at his dwelling place. The city sheriff and a squadron of soldiers rushed to his grimy residence, smashed down the door, and with burning brands descended to the dismal cellar. The oak trunk was set there, chained and padlocked. The sheriff approached it with the key that they had taken from around Jazeb's neck.

'It can't be killed,' he had told them while back on the rack with red hot irons hovering above his eye balls. 'But it can be stopped. Take out the eye! Take out the eye! It's the only way. But it must be set in stone in a holy place beneath the open sky, otherwise it will grow back. The eye will grow back and then my little beauty's work will begin again…'

In Jazeb's hovel an awful slobbering and sucking could be heard from the trunk, and claws scratched furiously upon bare wood. The Mal-Beast was starving for blood and fresh human brains, and could smell humans close by. Swords and daggers ready, the soldiers braced themselves for action as the brave sheriff unlocked the trunk. The Mal-Beast leapt out – black as night and as hairy as an ape, a single red eye glowing and glaring in the centre of its shaggy forehead. Long blade-like claws slashed at throats; razor teeth bit into legs and arms. Five of the soldiers were dead before the rest managed to pin the beast to the floor, ready for the deed. With a sharp intake of breath, the sheriff plunged his thumb and forefinger into the soft flesh around the creature's eye. He nipped firmly, got a pincer grip on the red jelly sphere, then ripped. With a slushy, popping sound the eye was plucked out, and the creature rendered harmless. In the celebration and congratulating following the eye-plucking, the Mal-Beast slithered away into the night, slinking like a wounded dog into the labyrinth of alleyways and ginnels. Mindful of Jazeb's last words - for indeed, the rigours of torture had proved too much for him - the glowing red eye was set into a stone, the stone placed in a slab, and slab set in a secret but holy place beneath the open sky.

It is said that even to this day, on the three nights of the full moon, York's own golem emerges from its hiding place in the heart of York and crawls about the city streets on all fours, feeling and scratching at the stone slabs, seeking its lost, single eye. The Mal-Beast no longer feeds on human brains, but survives these days on thrown-away fries, kebabs and pizzas, supplementing its street-food diet with Saturday night drunk-throw-ups and the occasional unlucky pigeon. Black as night, hairy as an ape, looking something akin to a large black dog, whimpering pitifully, it crawls on all fours, always seeking its lost, single red eye. The Sheriff, being cunning as well as brave, had other 'eyes' made up – spheres of glass, exact replicas of the ripped out eye. These were also set in the paving slabs around the city streets, with the intention of confusing the beast, and hopefully distracting it from locating its own real eye. For, should it find that eye set there in the pavement ...

'Twixt a high gate and a low gate,
Where Earth meets the Sky...',

... and should it manage to pluck that eye out of the stone slab, and should it set that eye back in the centre of its ape-like, shaggy forehead – well, the consequences are too terrible to consider. And especially for many of the good folk of York who are blood descendents of those whom participated in those terrible deeds at Clifford Tower back on that fateful day in 1190.

*

If, after reading this tale, you happen to visit York and decide to seek the Golem-eye out, and actually find it, please do not touch it, nor be tempted to pluck it from the holy slab where it is set. And, pray, please keep its whereabouts a total secret, as there are many around you on those very streets that would suffer the consequences of Jazeb's hell-bent evil intention to *'survive and avenge'* through his ever-living, dark, most malignant Mal-Beast.

PAD-PAD

Pad... pad... pad... pad.

'Don't sleep out in Mulgrave Woods. There's the Pad-Pad!'

Those were our Nana Morgan's words. But we were young, needed adventure, so of course we just ignored her. We went to the woods in the afternoon to play in the trees and streams there. Come twilight, when we were sure no rangers or game keepers were about to shoo us away home, we pitched our tents in a remote clearing by the old castle. My brother, my cousin, our neighbour and me, we slept out. We lit a camp-fire and enjoyed a summer's night in the gorgeous blackness of the woods. No Pad-Pad came to torment us that time.

The Pad-Pad. One third panther, one third goat, one third something resembling human. Or so Nana Morgan claimed. It was a true forest-beast, long lost now to the outside world, but she knew for sure that a family of them still thrived in the ancient heart of Mulgrave Woods. Evil, cruel, sadistic beasts, they were silent in the shadow of the forest, their only sound the pad-pad-pad of foot-tread as they closed in on their prey. That sound, then the awful, fang-bared howling just before they ripped into their victims.

Nana Morgan had told that to our Dad and Uncle Peter, and when she was old she told it to us grandchildren, trying to scare us with her gory stories.

'And what does Pad-Pad feed on, my loves?' Nana Morgan's wrinkled eyes widened as she told us: 'On mice and cats and rabbits and owl-young; on fairies and goblins. Oh… and on children. Yes, my little sweethearts. On your kind! On tiny, little frightened children! The Pad-Pad will come for you as sure as I'm sitting here!'

Old Nana Morgan died years ago now, but the Pad-Pad lives on beyond her wild story.

*

'You can't sleep out in the Mulgrave Woods! There's the Pad-Pad. And it's Halloween!'

Our Uncle Peter's words now. But our parents were young-hearted. They loved adventures. They didn't want us out trick-or-treating in the streets and alleyways of Whitby at night.

'Don't be daft, Pete,' our Mum told him. 'That's just Nana's nonsense. Anyway, we'll be with them. We're camping in the field just over the hill.'

Uncle Peter seemed angry then, and spoke as if holding back something secret from the ears of us children.

'You can't let them go, John. Tell her. You must both be mad. It's Halloween. The Pad-Pad. Remember that night – the Pad-Pad?!'

'Oh, stop it,' snapped Mum, taking Peter's arm, leading him toward the house door.

'You don't still really believe all that stuff, Peter? All that nonsense Nana Morgan used to spout.'

'The Pad-Pad,' she'd tell them – her neck quivering, the skin pimpled like uncooked chicken skin. 'They live in the woods. In the hollows in the woods. In the castle in the woods. In the tunnel in the woods. Stay there after sunset and call out its name – that'll be the last of you! Pad-Pad will have you! Mark my words.'

'It was all just nonsense,' Mum said. 'Old folk-tales. Listen Peter, we'd rather have our kids happy in the woods than roaming the streets with Halloween weirdoes!'

Uncle Peter shook his head.

'Pad-Pad,' he whispered. 'I wouldn't take my kids down there tonight, not for all the money in the world.'

He stormed from the house then, slamming the door. Mum sighed with relief. Dad lit the candle in the pumpkin. We packed food, torches, lanterns and firewood; me, our Sam, our cousin Martin and little Billy from down the road. We loaded the tents and sleeping bags into the car. We locked the door and checked the windows. At last we set off for Sandsend, and Mulgrave Woods.

*

'Whooo... Whoooh...'
We spooked weird noises through the darkness, imitating owls and squeaking bats.

'I used to be a werewolf but I'm all right nowwhoooooh!' I joked.

'Pad-Pad,' shouted cousin Martin. 'Pad-Pad. Come and get us, if you dare!'

'Ssh!' I hissed, thumping his arm. 'Shut up! Don't be so stupid.' The story was that to call out for the Pad-Pad would bring it down on you for sure – just like Bloody Mary in the mirror, or The Lawn Mower Man who comes through the wall.

The woods about us rustled, but our torches were bright. Mum and Dad were in their tent a few hundred yards away. We'd eaten hot dogs and marshmallows. We'd had diet coke and a sip of Dad's cold beer. We'd told spooky stories about babysitters, voodoo spells and freaky dolls. Black trees hissing in the breeze; the drone of the sea moans in the distance; Pad-Pad is out there in the darkness.
Halloween in the heart of Mulgrave Woods.
How much cooler can you get!?

Night blossoms to deeper blackness. Above the trees a silver moon floats its cruel, slanted smile. Stars swarm like angry wasps. Real owls hoot, making all of us jump. Our torches are still bright, but we are cold now. Suddenly we all goose-pimple with real fear.

Crick! Crack!
The snapping of twigs.
A footstep on dry leaves.
We stop breathing. We freeze. We listen.

'It's just Dad,' I say. 'He's mucking about.'

Though even I don't quite believe myself.
More rustling, then a louder
SNAP!

And now we are frightened, head hair prickling
'Dad?' shouts Sam, my younger brother. 'Dad? Mum? Stop mucking about!'
Sssnap. Snap. Pad. Pad.
We edge nearer to the embers of our camp-fire. There is a silence. Even the trees cease hissing. The sea's drone now is just a whisper. Then we hear it – a sort of soft breathing, quiet as the rustle of silky moth wings. There's movement out in the trees. Something is definitely creeping toward our tents!

Pad-pad-pad-pad… thudding footsteps, circling, slow-moving, pacing toward our camp.

'Dad!' I scream – he's gone too far with the joke this time, teasing us, trying to scare us like this. He's probably just sneaking up with a surprise pizza.

Pad… pad… pad…pad…
The strides stop just beyond the range of the camp-fire light. Our torches flash madly, picking out nothing but black shapes and shadows. Little Billy from down the road clutches onto my leg and begins to whimper. Hoping that this really is just them mucking about, I manage to tremble out:
'Mu-um? Dad? Stop it now and get over here into the light.'

A pause. Just silence. Then something is sprinting toward us, a shape rushing out of the darkness.

'Run!' it screams. 'To the car park. Now! Run for your lives!'

It's a familiar voice. Uncle Peter's. But he sounds different – screeching – terrified. And there in the light of the camp-fire I see that he's covered in blood. In his hand he has a knife. His face is raked with bleeding scratches, his shirt and trousers ripped to shreds.

'Pad-Pad!' he screams. 'Run from the Pad-Pad!'

And we run, blindly, screaming, stumbling in mud, tumbling in ditches, ploughing through streams without a thought of their depth or slippery treachery. And always, just behind us, the breath on our shoulders, the graze of fangs and the horrible foot-fall: Pad-pad! Pad-pad! Pad-pad! Pad-Pad!

We make it to the car park. The sea gleams like silver milk across the beach, hissing white foam upon the sands. We make it to the car, gasping, lungs hurting from the sprint. There's me ... there's Sam... there's cousin Martin... there's little Billy from down the road. At last, Uncle Peter ... shirt shredded... covered in blood... and behind us...

around… the awful echo… Pad-Pad Pad-Pad Pad-Pad. Then another noise swelling, shrilling, piercing through the banging my own blood-beat. Whar...whar...whar…whar…

A siren. Blaring, screeching closer. A suddenly welcoming and hopeful sound. Of all things, a siren - I never thought I could be so comforted by that awful wail. We laugh and hug, weeping a cheer, so relieved to see the blue flashing lights. Only Uncle Peter is silent, standing away by the trees. He's staring back into the blackness of those terrible woods, going back in, slashing at the dark with his razor-edged knife.

*

'Don't sleep out in Mulgrave Woods!' I say.
I say it now to all our children. I'm horrified at the thought that their parents might let them stray.

'There's the Pad-Pad,' I say. 'Pad-Pad. One third panther, one third goat, one third something resembling…' I don't finish the sentence. It can't be human. I can't bring myself to say the human.

'My own Mum and Dad,' I say, but can't continue.
Our Mum. Our Dad. And Uncle Peter.
The Pad-Pad snatched them *all* from us on that murderous night.

CRACKS

The year 2000 passed without the world ending in chaos because of "the millennium bug". Life beyond 2000 went on as usual - eating, sleeping, school, work, shopping.

In the early 2000's the world did not burn up due to green house gasses or the spreading hole in the upper ozone layer. Life went on - eating, sleeping, shopping, texting.

The comets and asteroids that were due to strike earth between 2007 - 2010 all missed by several hundred thousand miles. Life went on - shopping, eating, Facebook, tweeting.

It seemed that at every turn the predictions of the end of the world were wrong. Even the eagerly awaited 'end of time' predicted by the Mayan calendar in 2012 was a disappointment. Nothing happened. The planets did not collide. The hand of God did not emerge from the sky to punch the world to smithereens. Everything went on just as normal. For a while.

Danny and Lisa were both 14, and were in love. They went everywhere together and their parents had long since stopped trying to keep them apart.

'They'll snap out of it,' Danny's parents said.

'It'll all fall apart soon,' Lisa's folks replied.

'Cracks will appear in the relationship,' their friends predicted enviously.

'We'll love each other until the end of time,' Danny and Lisa swore, and swapped sloppy kisses.

Danny and Lisa laughed when they first heard the news on television.

'The world actually appears to be ending,' the lady newsreader casually announced. 'According to scientific reports, the very fabric of the universe is actually cracking into tiny fragments.'

'Oh yeah, tell us another one,' snorted Danny.

'Just look at her weird blouse,' Lisa laughed, pointing at the screen. The newsreader wore a purple and yellow blob patterned blouse with puffy sleeves and a huge collar. 'End of the world or not, her blouse is the real tragedy here.'

They chuckled and snuggled closer on the settee, gazing into each others eyes. When none of their mates were around, they liked to pretend they were Romeo and Juliet. *Even if the world was to end tomorrow*, they swore, lips poised for a kiss, *their undying love would live forever*. Just then Danny's dad walked in, so they leapt up and headed off to The Mall for a burger and coke.

Few people took the world-ending news seriously. Lisa was a Science Fiction fan though, with an interest in hard science, alien invasions and world-domination conspiracy theories. She was a reader of The Fortean Times magazine. She didn't believe that men had really landed on the moon - it was all faked in a film studio. UFO's were real and lizard aliens who shape-shifted into politicians actually ruled the world. Every mobile phone was a camera and microphone, monitoring and tracking you, recording everything you did or said. Nothing was as it seemed, she was sure about that. She knew all about The Illuminati, Slender Man and Shadow People. Through reading many stories about space journeys and time-travel, Lisa was familiar with sub-atomic core particle decay theories and the inverse time lapse continuum. Despite sneering at the world-ending news, when away from Danny she trawled the net, read all the newspapers and watched strange late night news programmes. She began to pore and frown over news articles, even when Danny was around. He thought that she was losing it. He was secretly a bit jealous about her new interest - when she was reading she went for hours without sending him a text or bringing him a biscuit. It was just too much for him when she spent a whole afternoon googling for information about 'inverse unravelling string theories'.

'Give me a kiss, Lisa,' he said, watching her

fingers dance and click over the keyboard.

'Hang on a minute until this file downloads.'

'What's up with you, angel?' he crooned, stroking her newly furrowed brow. 'You aren't turning all intellectual on me, are you?'

'There might be something in it, that's all,' she said, pulling away from his fingers. 'It's all to do with universal electron failure. Listen Danny, it says here that using ultra-high frequency electron telescopes, scientists have detected fibre thin flaws throughout the structure of the universe. Microcracks, they're calling them. They're caused by the universe contracting as end-time reverses. They're visible. And they're everywhere, from the most distant corner of the universe right down to ... well, this very room.'

She looked up. Danny was gaping at her, shaking his head. He hated it when she talked like a science teacher. She took his astonishment to mean that he was confused by her big words.

'It's a bit like a power failure,' she simplified for him. 'Or having your electricity supply cut off.'

Danny was still mightily unimpressed. He could hardly believe it - his lovely girlfriend was turning into a geek before his very eyes.

'Come on,' he said. 'I've got to get you out of here before you lose it completely.'

He persuaded her to shut down the computer then took her down to The Mall for a burger and an ice cream drink.

Despite Danny's teasing, Lisa still scanned all the newspapers, but all articles on the world-ending seemed to have stopped being printed. There was rarely even a mention of it on television, and all the 'world cracks' web-sites were suddenly closed down. Lisa suspected that the world's political leaders had consulted each other about the crisis. To avoid mass panic and disorder they had secretly agreed on an international media blackout about the disaster. The whole 'cracking' story was dismissed as a hoax. More important issues such as royal babies and political scandals once again became the leading news items.

Earth's final summer was a hot one. On an evening after school, Lisa would sit out in the garden with a cool drink, her newspapers and pad. She was still searching for articles that mentioned the universal micro-cracks. Behind her back her school friends, and sometimes Danny, had taken to calling her *Lisa Einstein* and *Lisa-geek*. Week after week there was nothing in the papers or on the net, then one sunny afternoon a tiny article at the bottom of a page grabbed her attention.

'***Big Mountain Vanishes!***' it declared. Then

went on: *'Mount Everest, once the world's highest mountain, is no longer there, a group of climbers claimed today. The disappointed British climbers, just back from Nepal...'*

'Here, Danny, listen to this!' she yelped out. He was at the bottom of the garden, messing about at basketball with his mates. She read the article out to them, but they shrugged. Lisa scanned the sky. Through her ultra-violet shades, she was sure that she could make out a faint web of hairline cracks criss-crossing the blue. She remembered reading that the biggest things would not necessarily be the first to disintegrate. The pattern of collapse would by its nature be chaotic. A mountain here, a flower there, then a building, next a distant star. A thought occurred to her and she stood up from the sun lounger, peering around the sky, searching for something there.

'Hey,' she called out uneasily, 'When was the last time any of you lot saw the moon?'

Danny laughed again, but was also uneasy. Lisa's behaviour was embarrassing him in front of his mates.

'Don't worry about Lisa,' he muttered, 'I think she's cracking up.'

But the moon had vanished, and each night a few more stars went out in the ever darkening sky. Mountains dissolved; flowers disintegrated; islands disappeared. Before long the first whole city had collapsed into tiny fragments and blown away as dust. When buildings and objects simply vanished in every street of every town of the world, it was no longer possible for the governments to deny that universal disintegration was not a hoax. The panic though was not as widespread as had been predicted. Most people tried to get on with their normal lives – sleeping, eating, tweeting, shopping. But all the world now waited for the inevitable end of everything.

To celebrate the forthcoming end of the world, both Danny and Lisa borrowed a hundred pounds from their parents. They wanted to use the money on new outfits, and to treat their mates to a pizza and a night of ten-pin bowling. They were dressed up and almost ready to go, Lisa just having a final check of her make-up in the bathroom mirror.
  'Come on, Lisa. You look beautiful,' Danny crooned. Of late he had been showering her with chocolates and roses, and trying to say all the right things. He felt guilty about the names he had been calling her behind her back when it turned out that she had been right all along.
  'Won't be a minute,' she shouted. She was finding it difficult to see her face in the mirror, which seemed to be hazy and misted over from within. The glass was criss-crossed with faint lines,

like a cracked car windscreen.

'Danny,' she murmured around her lip-stick. 'This mirror - it's all cracked...'

Her voice sounded strange in her own ears, and with a lurch of her heart she realised what was happening. Danny came floating toward her, his anxious face also criss-crossed with tiny cracks. They froze there. They stared hopelessly at each other, both fading. As they fragmented away into dust and particles before each other's very eyes they both managed to mouth out the words, *'I love you.'*

The Beast of Bay*

Jet black,
Slick sheen of coals,
Amber eyes embers
Set deep in black holes;
Watching, weighing,
Surveying night's prey,
Half legend, half nightmare;
The Beast of Bay.

Claws laser razors,
Teeth cold glinting steel
To grip and snap the quarry's spine –
No time to squeal.
One cold precise claw flick -
Warm prey disembowelled
Then the murmur of cat-feasting,
No victory howled.

Quick, melt away!
Back to pitch of midnight,
Shadow - always out there
On the edge of our sight,
Stalking down fox, dog, rabbit
And lamb;
By the time that we've glimpsed it – already gone.

Speed of silent starlight,
Strength of coldest fear.
The Beast of Bay!
The Beast,
 Is bolting...
 It's here!

*A mythical panther like creature that is regularly sighted around Robin Hood's Bay and Whitby, North Yorkshire.

Other titles available for young people by Chris Firth through Electraglade Press:

'**Strip 1**' – desert island survival story – on a traffic island! (kindle)

'**Ghost Stories From Whitby - The Mulgrave Tales**' - ghosts and ghouls (paperback and kindle)

'**The Electraglade Tales**' – futuristic short stories/ Arts Council England Writer's Award winning collection (paperback and kindle)

Made in the USA
Charleston, SC
21 August 2014